PETS FOR SALE

by Rita Golden Gelman

Illustrated by Fredr...

SCHOLASTIC INC.

New York Toronto London Auckland Sydney

Por Pily, Raúl, y mi amigo, Ruly.

R.G.G.

For Sally and Erik

F.W.

ISBN 0-590-33641-X

Text copyright © 1986 by S&R Gelman Associates, Inc.
Illustrations copyright © 1986 by Fredric Winkowski.
All rights reserved. Published by Scholastic Inc.
HELLO READER is a trademark of Scholastic Inc.
Art direction by Diana Hrisinko.
Text design by Theresa Fitzgerald.

12 11 10 9 8 7 6 5 4 3   6 7 8 9/8 0 1/9

"HEY WHO?
HEY ME?"

"I have some pets
that you should see.

Flat pets.
Hat pets.
Pets that bite.
Pets that wake you up at night.
Pets that cry.
Pets that spy.

Have you found a pet to buy?"

"NOT I!"

"I have pets that grin all day.
And dizzy pets that spin all day.
Pets that swear.
Pets that scare.
Quiet pets that like to stare.

Well now,
have you picked a pet?"

"NOT YET."

"These pets like to sit a lot.
These pets like to spit a lot.

This one likes to slam the door."

**"I THINK I'D LIKE TO
LOOK SOME MORE."**

"I have a pet
that loves to clean

your room,
your tub,
your hair.

He has a friend that messes up.
You have to
buy the pair."

"This one likes to jump
on beds,
and write on walls,
and sit on heads.

She bangs on pots.
She does that best.
This pet's a prize."

"THAT PET'S
A PEST!"

"These pets like to
roll down hills.
But they are
very lazy.

Surely you will
take a few?"

"DO YOU THINK
I'M CRAZY?"

"Here's a pet that blows balloons,
a million every day.

And here's a pet that pops them
so they don't get in the way.
Take one home.
Take two,
take three.
Take them all!"

"OH NO, NOT ME!"

"This one likes to scream and yell.
He does it loud.
He does it well.
His dragon-breath is red and hot.

Take him home."

"I'D RATHER NOT!"

"Here's a tiny
little thing
who loves to punch,

and pinch,

and sting.

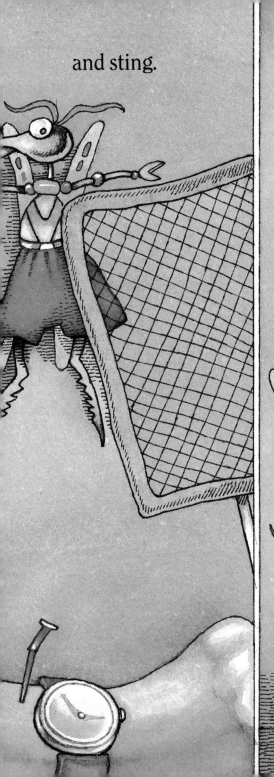

He also does a
silly dance.
Will you take him?"

"NOT A CHANCE!"

"This one likes to smash your cakes,
and spill your milk,
and steal your steaks.
She's very smart.
She's very cheap."

"I DO NOT WANT HER.
SHE'S A CREEP!"

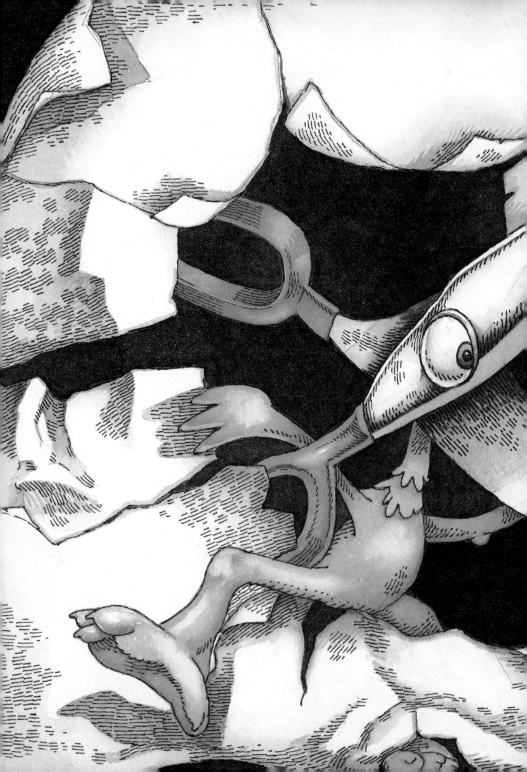

"This one likes to cut and glue,
your books,
your shirts,
your pants,
and you!

See how fast he glues and cuts?
I'm sure you want him."

"ARE YOU NUTS?"

"This little pet
        will brush your hair,
        and tie your shoes,
        and rock your chair.
She also snuggles
if you let her."

"I DO NOT THINK
I WANT TO
PET HER."

"This one eats the foods you hate.
  And takes the blame when you are late.

  She says, 'God bless you,' when you sneeze.

  He scratches itches,
      patches knees.
  These pets are nice as you can see."

"IT'S TRUE THEY'RE NICE.
  BUT NOT FOR ME."

"That's all my pets.
I have no more.
Except the one
behind that door.

She doesn't clean.
She doesn't grin.
She doesn't spit or
spy or spin.
She doesn't cut.
She doesn't glue.
This pet is not
the pet for you."